Dear Ewan,

Happy Reading!! :)

Best,

[illegible]

by Alison Kelly & Matt Millard

# Contents

# About the Book

*Come into the park. There's a world of adventure inside!*

When Detective Sergeant Goldie and Constable Manny are asked to investigate the disappearance of a duckling and the swan Prince, it's the start of an exciting adventure through the wild!

Before they know it, they find themselves fighting herons and a mysterious new leader!

Will they find the missing animals?...

The race is on!

For All the Wonderful Animals of Kelsey Park

# DUCK STORY:

## *The Lost Eagle*

By

ALISON KELLY & MATT MILLARD

# CHAPTER 1 - AMAZONIA

Hector, the Harpy Eagle, soared through the pale blue sky. With his sleek grey, black and white feathers, ferocious green eyes, and an exuberant tuft of facial feathers, he really was a *spectacular* bird of prey.

Harpy Eagles are among the world's largest and most powerful eagles and Hector was no exception. His home was the magnificent rainforest, or "*Amazonia,*" as it was known by the animals who lived there.

Hector was a skilled hunter. He'd killed hundreds of sloth bears, monkeys and large birds in his time. But recently his kills had been fewer and fewer as humans had been clearing the forest's trees, and many of the animals were leaving.

As he was one of the biggest birds, Hector was known as the "Bird King of the Jungle." All the other animals cowered when they saw him and ran from his shadow. Hector was proud they were afraid of him, his very survival depended upon it.

He turned and dived down through the clouds, the cool air ruffling his feathers. Faster and faster he flew until he soared above the endless canopy of billions of trees. He glided through them until he reached his own tree, his home.

Hector's nest was high up in one of the tallest trees in the jungle, a Brazil nut tree, on the banks of the river. He and his mate, Ana, had built the nest using hundreds of sticks and branches, as well as plants and animal fur from his many kills.

Ana proudly perched in their nest. Beside her sat their three hungry chicks *squawking*. Their mouths open wide with excitement for the tasty morsels their papa had brought them.

Ana greeted Hector eagerly, until she saw that his huge talons were empty, *again*.

'*Where* is the food? You *know* we have a hungry brood!' she crowed, her eyes flashing angrily.

Hector sighed and mumbled to himself as he turned around. He knew better than to argue with his mate, after all, she *was* bigger than him. So, Hector launched himself back into the air and flew through the thick fog that sat above the trees as he continued his search for something big and juicy.

*That wasn't there before...* he thought, with anticipation.

His eagle eyes narrowed to focus on a sloth bear clinging to a tree. A second later, he turned mid-flight and swooped down in the unsuspecting creature's direction, talons at the ready.

A few minutes later, Hector triumphantly returned to his nest with the wriggling sloth bear. Ana and the chicks jumped up and down with excitement when they saw him.

'Papa, Papa!' chirped the happy chicks.

But just as he was about to dish out their dinner, he heard a sound, the ominous crunch of twigs on the ground.

Hector's head turned, and there hidden amongst the trees was a *human*! Hector was a master at evading humans. But he'd seen *this* human before. He realised, in horror, that the human was tracking him.

'Stay down!' Hector squawked at his family. 'I'll lead them away from you!'

He turned to see that the human had disappeared. 'Don't leave us, Hector!' Ana cried.

'Papa, Papa!' yelped the terrified chicks.

'Trust me,' Hector said to his little family. 'I'll lead the human away and I'll be back.'

He hurriedly flapped his wings as he rose through the trees. He'd almost escaped when…

*POW!*

Pain shot through his body and Hector fell from the sky.

As he fell, he heard his chicks cry out his name. Ana's anguished *squawks* echoed through the jungle.

*At least they were safe*, was his last thought before everything went *BLACK*.

When Hector awoke, he had a painful wing and a groggy head. It took a while for his eyes to adjust to the dim light, and there was a strange *buzzing sound* all around him.

Hector stumbled forwards and bumped into something. He lifted his claw and closed it around a cage. Hector didn't know what it was, or *where* he was. He tried to open his wings, but he was trapped. The strange cage surrounded him.

Hector *squawked* in terror.

'Be quiet!' came a voice from the darkness.

A man stalked towards Hector and kicked the cage. Hector shrank back in the corner when he realised it was the man who'd captured him.

'Bad bird!' shouted the man.

Hector glared up at him in brooding silence. The man glared back.

'You'll learn,' he said, wickedly, before walking away.

Fear and tiredness swept over Hector. Little did he know that as he slept, he was going on the flight of his life, to a *new home* thousands of miles away from his family and everything he had ever known.

**The next day…**

# CHAPTER 2 - THE OWL & THE OTHERS

The wind *whistled* and *howled* above a huge, red brick castle on the coast of Scotland. The castle had small grey turrets and towers which faced the Atlantic Ocean.

Four large hounds guarded the castle, stalking the acres of rugged land that surrounded it.

In a room inside the castle, Hector stared out of a cage gloomily, his long talons hooked into the rails, and he shook them angrily. ***The back talons of a Harpy Eagle can grow up to 5 inches long–longer than a grizzly bear's claws!***

Hector was surrounded by other caged birds. But his cage was the largest, as he was the *biggest* bird of them all, of course.

'Let! Me! Out!' Hector shouted.

'Why am I here? I haven't done anything wrong!' He paced around his cage angrily. *Screeching* and *squawking, banging* and *bashing* his claws and wings against the rails.

'I don't know *why* you want to waste your time. You've only been here five minutes,' came a small voice from the next cage.

Hector turned to see a small Short-eared owl with bright-yellow eyes and mottled brown feathers staring at him. Hector glared down his hooked beak at the owl, it looked like it'd been there forever.

'Crying and squawking is futile,' the owl said. 'They'll never let you out. So, you might as well get used to it like everyone else has,' the owl declared.

'I'm not like everyone else!' Hector *bellowed.*

He tried to raise his magnificent wings to show them, but the cage was too small.

'Aren't you?' asked the owl.

Hector *bashed* his head against the rails. But he stopped when the human came into the room. One by one, the owl and the others were wheeled out. Hector soon learnt that they spent their days performing tricks and displays in shows for the humans.

They were the entertainment!

Hector watched with disgust as they flew backwards and forwards, landing onto the gloved hand of the man who'd caught him. Hector was the only one left behind because *he* refused to perform.

One afternoon, after a show, the owl came to the side of Hector's cage and stared at him.

'I've been questioning humans for years,' he hooted as he continued with widening eyes. 'Why do they like to see us suffer in these cages? Do they like seeing us homesick? Are we more humane than them? Did *we* do something *wrong*?'

Hector stared back at him. 'NO!' the owl hooted loudly.

'We didn't do *anything* wrong. They just take what *they* want. You're a show bird now, one of us. Get used to it,' he commanded.

'I'll *never* be like *you*,' Hector spat.

The owl looked at him with mild curiosity.

'Don't be a twit! A word of advice,' he tooted. 'If they don't have a use for you, they'll *lose* you. You'll *never* get out of this cage alive.'

He looked over at some stuffed owls and birds that sat on a shelf on the other side of the room.

Hector swallowed.

'What do they want?' he asked, disturbed.

'What all humans want, entertainment.' The owl drawled as he lifted his wings and gave a flamboyant wave of his feathers.

Hector stared past the owl and out of the window at the trees in the castle grounds. They reminded him of home. Oh, how he longed to be there now.

'Back home, they took the trees and now they're taking *us*,' Hector said. 'Soon I suppose they'll take our chicks.'

'Don't have any!' said the owl with a hoot. 'Too noisy!' he *guffawed* at his own joke.

Hector *laughed* for the first time in a long time. But then he thought of his *own* chicks and his beloved mate, Ana. He wondered if they were okay.

Would he ever see them again? Would they survive without him?

He held back tears of anger and frustration as he thought about his family being unable to protect themselves. But Ana was a survivor; he was sure she'd find a way until he got back home.

*Ahhh, home...*

He closed his beady eyes and recalled the scent. He imagined flying over the green-topped trees that stretched as far as the eye could see. He used to perch on top of the tallest tree and watch as the rain poured down, the leaves looked like glimmering lights.

Hector longed for his home. He longed for his family.

And he longed for his *life* the way it was *before.*

Hector's anger grew and grew.

*'I'm going back!'* he snarled fiercely.

'Perhaps,' said the owl. 'But only if you *learn to play* the game.'

Hector watched the owl walk over to his perch and sit down. He closed his eyes and went to sleep with a gentle *snore.*

*'Learn to play the game.'*

Hector would play the game until he could escape.

The next day, when the man came to collect the owl and the others, he walked past Hector's cage. Usually, Hector would ignore him and *squawk*, but on this day, something unusual happened - Hector was as silent as a mouse.

The man watched him warily, then moved towards him tentatively. He slowly opened Hector's cage. Hector did nothing. He stood perfectly still and allowed the man to place metal cuffs around his neck and feet.

'See. Told you you'd learn,' the man *sneered.*

That morning Hector was taken out to train. A week later, he performed in his first show. The audience made a deafening ***ROAR*** when he took his first dive.

Of course, Hector thought about escaping, but the man put an electronic tag around his ankle before each show. The owl said that the man could use it to find him if he escaped.

It wasn't long before Hector became the number one attraction in the castle because of his incredible lunges and dives. The humans *clapped* and *roared* at every turn he took in the sky.

*No one had ever seen a Harpy Eagle before.* The very sight of him alone drew people from around the country who marvelled at his strange feathers and the amazing feats he could perform.

But Hector *hated* performing.

He hated the way they were all rolled out in their cages. He realised the other birds weren't as special as him. He looked at the wise, old owl - hardly anyone clapped for him anymore.

Hector felt sad for him, but he pushed the feeling away as he waited for the sun to go down.

That evening, while the other birds were asleep, Hector crept to the front of his cage. Each night he'd been secretly picking the lock with his talon, and tonight he was close to succeeding.

Hector held his breath when the door swung open. He ripped off the electronic tag around his ankle and walked out of his prison. He crept past the wise old owl, who opened an eye.

Hector stopped and held his breath.

They *both* knew that one HOOT from the owl and he was done for. Hector waited for the owl to raise the alarm, but instead the owl winked and closed his eye.

With relief, Hector hopped down onto the floor. There was a window open in the room, so he jumped onto the ledge, nudged it open with his wing and launched himself into the air.

The hounds in the gardens below caught Hector's scent and ran towards his fleeing figure. But Hector swooped down over them and gave a *WHOOP!* of triumph as they ferociously *barked* at his retreating figure.

The sky was stormy and grey, and the rolling clouds loomed over Hector like a shadow. He dived down the side of the castle, glided over a clifftop and soared over the North Sea.

As he flew away, he gave one last look back at the castle, now a tiny dot on the horizon. He thought about the owl and the others, and how they would surely spend the rest of their lives there. He felt sad for them.

But Hector was grateful he had his freedom. If he could stay alive, he would find his way back to his family. He flew night and day, faster than the wind. As he flew, he marvelled at the purple, brown and green colours of the Scottish Highlands.

He flew through storms and rain, eager to create as much distance as he could from the castle. A few hours later, he reached another unknown land called England.

TWIT TWOO!!!

# CHAPTER 3 - KELSEY PARK

After hours of flying, Hector needed to rest. He circled over an abundance of green and blue, then swooped down and came to a stop inside a park with a huge, sparkling lake. Kelsey Park, a beautiful oasis in the town of Beckenham, Kent.

The park was green and full of vibrant colours. There were hundreds of varieties of trees, plants and flowers that Hector had never seen before. Even some of the animals were unusual.

On one side of the lake was a magnificent white and silver palace where the Swan Royal family lived. There was a small waterfall with a stream that led to an overgrown island inhabited by herons on the other side of the lake.

Hector spent the next few days hiding in the bushes, sampling the local delicacies. He stalked the shadows eating a small animal or two a day and watching the goings on inside the park.

He saw the Swan King and Queen, the park royalty, and their four young cygnets. Much fuss was made of the eldest cygnet, Prince George, who seemed prone to getting into trouble.

Hector noticed how the royals were protected by a legion of Canadian and Egyptian Geese soldiers. But the obstinate, young Prince seemed to keep giving them the slip and often disappeared to swim around areas of the park he wasn't allowed to go to.

He watched one other animal closely. One-eyed Billy, the scrawny and shifty leader of the herons. Hector discovered that the herons spent their days stalking the edges of the lake watching for ducklings and other younglings.

Hector watched them steal some ducklings. He shook his head. They had such little imagination. If *he* were Billy, he would be far more interested in ruling the kingdom.

A plan began to form inside his mind. If he could gain control of the park, he could gain control of the geese soldiers. Hector knew they migrated to North America, perhaps he could migrate with them, maybe they knew the way back home?

But how to get control of the park?

Hector watched Prince George give his guards the slip again. He moved closer through the bushes and watched him. A while later, the King flew out of the palace and over to his son.

'What is wrong with you George! How many times do I have to tell you, you need your guards! You're the son of the King who will one day BE King!' he hissed as he flew off leaving a stern-looking goose to march his son home.

Hector smiled, the answer to his problems had just appeared….

# CHAPTER 4 - THE DUCKLING

Detective Sergeant Michael Gold, or "Goldie," as he was known, yawned at his desk. He was tired from the busy night before. He rubbed his eyes and stared down at his cold cup of coffee.

Goldie was a duck with golden feathers and a dark yellow beak. As the Pond Police's star police officer, it was well-known that Goldie solved the cases the others couldn't.

The Pond Police patrolled every corner of Kelsey Park, including the woodland, water ways, Swan Kingdom and Puddletown, the city centre in the heart of the park.

This morning alone, Goldie had solved a case involving a Kingfisher who'd broken a window at the Swan Palace and single-handedly stopped a feud between rival gangs of rats and squirrels who were fighting over a missing batch of nuts.

All in all, it'd been a very productive morning and now it was time for breakfast, a pond weed latte and a seeded bagel.

Goldie waddled away from the Pond Police Headquarters. The headquarters was a huge tree with hundreds of branches sticking up in every direction.

The tree was on the edge of the lake with two red slides the police officers used to shoot into the water whenever there were emergencies. But Goldie never used the slides anymore - in his mind, they were for the younger officers.

As he walked through the park, he saw a lone, young duckling running towards him. Goldie headed towards her just as a Mandarin duck family tumbled out of the bushes behind her.

'Get back here, Jess!' called Patrick Green, the father of the family.

He was a handsome duck with a red bill and a large white crescent above his eyes. He had a red face and whiskers. On his breast were purple and white feathers, and on his back were two, large orange feathers stuck up like boat sails.

Patrick was with his wife, Anne, and their adorable yellow and brown ducklings, Kurt, Harrison, Kayleigh and Valentina. Kurt and Harrison were squabbling, as usual.

'Morning, Detective Goldie!' said Patrick, a little flustered.

'Morning folks! Mrs Green,' Goldie quacked as he tipped his hat at her.

'So, these are the new young ones?' he asked. Patrick nodded. He reached Jess and poked his wing at her.

'You're in big trouble, young duckling!' He looked at Goldie. 'This one's always wandering off and getting lost!'

Jess ignored her father and ran up to Goldie. 'Are you a Pond Police officer?' she chirped excitedly. Goldie nodded. 'Do you go down the slides?' she asked seriously.

Goldie laughed. 'I try to avoid it, a bit too many feathers around the middle!' he said with a chuckle. 'And besides, I'm too old for that!' Patrick and Anne laughed.

'Where are you folks headed?' Goldie asked.

'We're on our way home. We just had breakfast in Puddletown, when Jess here waddled off,' Anne said with a raised eyebrow.

Goldie was solemn. 'She looks like trouble,' he said. 'You be careful, young Jess. This park may be big and beautiful, but it's also full of animals that are much bigger than you, and *some* of them might mean you harm.'

'Yeah, they'll EAT you!' Kurt interrupted.

Anne shushed him, and the family said their 'Goodbyes' and carried on their way.

The Green family lived on the other side of the park in a great oak tree. When they reached home, Anne put the ducklings down for a nap.

'When they wake up, I'm going to surprise them with a flying lesson,' Anne whispered to Patrick.

'Okay, darling, but be careful and watch out for Jess. Don't forget, after work I'm off to the Feathered Friends for a pint of Snail Ale,' he said with a chuckle. He kissed Anne on the cheek and stepped out of their tree hole.

A few hours later, Jess awoke beneath Anne's wing. She was warm and comfy and didn't intend on moving for many hours. But a few minutes later, her mother gently shook her awake.

'Right, come on you lot, wake up! It's time to fly the nest!' said Anne with a wink. The rest of the ducklings groaned as they woke up.

'Come on mum,' Harrison moaned.

But Anne ignored their pleas and waddled over to the tree hole where she flew out into the afternoon sky.

'Where's she gone?' said Jess in panic.

'It's time to practice flying, Jess,' chirped Valentina.

Jess watched as Harrison confidently waddled over to the tree hole and, without a backwards glance, he too launched himself outside.

***Although they were only 12 days old, it was usual for Mandarin ducklings to take to flight early.***

Jess gulped. Her feathers started to ruffle, and she was getting flustered as she waited for her turn. One by one, the others took turns to fly until there was only one duckling left.

Jess waddled over to the tree hole and peered out. She gasped.

She trembled as she stared down at her family. They called up to her with peeps and quacks of encouragement.

'I can't!' she tweeted.

She hugged her wings against her body and trembled as she heard her mother call to her from down below.

'Come on, Jess. Be brave, use your wings!' called Anne.

Jess knew they were all waiting for her. Finally, she took a deep breath, stepped forwards and threw herself out of the tree hole head first.

Unlike her siblings, who'd floated down gently, Jess fell through the air clumsily. As she fell, she hit her head on the branches and tried to steady herself with her tiny wings, but her body kept rolling as she tumbled through the air.

Finally, she landed on a patch of moss and leaves with a massive thud. 'Owww!' she yelped out.

Anne and Jess's siblings ran over to her. 'Are you alright, Jess?' Anne asked with concern. Anne checked Jess over and tenderly pecked her on the head.

Leaves in a nearby bush rustled. Anne looked at the bush cautiously. 'Come on, father's waiting, and we won't be safe until we reach the lake.'

The ducklings chirped with excitement. But Anne was a little worried. It's dangerous for ducklings to go into the water when they're so young, as they're at risk from herons and other predators.

One by one, they waddled behind their mother, not noticing the shadowy figure watching them from the bushes.

But Jess sensed something and stopped. Easily distracted, she turned and saw a pair of eyes staring back at her from the bushes.

Jess stared back.

Curious, she waddled towards the bushes, oblivious to the heron who'd silently dropped from the sky to swoop her up. The heron caught Jess by her wing and flew off.

The pair of eyes disappeared.

The Mandarin family reached the lake.

‘Right, my little ones,’ said Patrick, who did a quick count of the ducklings. He frowned. ‘Where’s Jess?’

Anne turned, her eyes filled quickly with worry.

The family re-traced their steps through the park. They searched the tree hole, but it was empty. They scoured the bushes and the hedgerows. For the rest of the day, they searched high and low, but Jess was nowhere to be found.

As the sun fell beneath the trees, a huge shadow of a bird passed over them. Patrick looked up, but the bird was gone.

On the other side of the park, in a gnarled horse chestnut tree, another animal saw the bird. Stumpy, a grey squirrel with half a tail, sat on his balcony as the giant shadow passed over him.

He stood up to get a better look but in a split second, it was gone.

# CHAPTER 5 - POND POLICE

Chief Inspector Quackovitz, the Pond Police's "big cheese", waddled into Goldie's office with a young, Mandarin duck recruit, trailing after her. Goldie sighed and looked back down at his paperwork; the Chief had obviously brought him another unwanted rookie partner.

Quackovitz was a small, black and white Tufted Duck. She was loud, uptight and generally angry all the time. In fact, Goldie couldn't recall a day when she wasn't quacking at some poor animal.

'How's the wing?' asked Quackovitz casually.

Goldie looked up from his paperwork. 'Fine,' he said grumpily. His eyes narrowed when he noticed the rookie staring at him.

'This young Mandarin is our newest recruit, Constable Manny,' said Quackovitz.

Manny stepped forward. 'I just want to say sir,' he began, 'I'm a big fan of yours, big fan, and I'm so excited…'

But before he could continue, Goldie held up a wing.

'I don't need any more partners,' he said dismissively before looking back down at his paperwork.

Quackovitz sighed and squawked angrily, her black and white feathers ruffled on top of her head and her eyes bulged.

'This isn't a request!' she quacked loudly with anger. '*This* is your new partner, and *here's* your new case.' She tossed a yellow file onto Goldie's desk.

'The father just reported her missing. And a few other younglings have also been reported missing today, but it could just be a coincidence… however, we need our BEST detective on the case. Now get to it!' she finished.

Without giving Goldie a chance to decline, Quackovitz waddled out of the office as fast as her short legs could move.

Goldie's eyes shot sideways. In Pond Police terms, a yellow file meant "MISSING DUCKLING."

Goldie hadn't worked on a missing duckling case since the previous summer.

Manny opened his beak, but Goldie held up his wing again and picked up the file. He quickly scanned its contents.

**MISSING DUCKLING REPORT**:
**Date**: 1/2/2020
**Name**: Jess Green
**Height**: 5cm
**Weight**: 1 pound
**Age**: 12 days old
**Breed**: Mandarin Duckling
**Eyes**: Brown
**Feathers**: Yellow with brown stripes
**Last Seen**: Near Heron Island

When he'd finished reading, Goldie pulled a photo from the file and shoved it in his pocket. He jumped to his webbed feet and hurried towards the door where he glanced back at Manny.

'Keep up!' he quacked 'I know this duckling.'

Goldie hurried down the corridor and stepped through a tree hole. For the first time in years, he slid down the red slides that shot him into the lake. Manny zoomed down the slide after him.

'Woo hoo, hooooo!!' he shouted. 'I've always wanted to do that!' he said excitedly as he splashed into the water.

POND
POLICE

Goldie shook his head and swam off across the lake.

A few minutes later, the mismatched partners emerged from the water and stood beneath a high-rise apartment block inside a horse chestnut tree.

There were small windows dotted along the edges with red and brown roof turrets.

'Why are we here?' Manny asked.

'This is Stumpy's home,' quacked Goldie. 'He's a fruit and nut trader, and he's also one of my most reliable informants. He's a bit of a wheeler-dealer, but he's got eyes and ears on the ground everywhere, so let *me* do all the quacking.'

Stumpy's grandad let the detectives in. 'He's in the living room, watching TV,' said the old, grey squirrel.

The detectives waddled into Stumpy's small living room. It was decorated with wallpaper with palm trees on it. The wallpaper, the curtains and the carpet all clashed with bright patterns and colours, but it was still a cosy home.

Stumpy was a grey squirrel in his mid-teens. He was sprawled across a tatty, flowery sofa with his paws dangling off the edge. He was wearing a vest covered in flamingos, and he popped acorns in his mouth as he watched "The Great Nut Bake Off."

Goldie coughed to announce their presence, Stumpy looked over. 'Detective Goldie. We're not meant to meet till next week?' he asked curiously, as he popped some more nuts in his mouth.

His eyes flicked to Manny, then back at Goldie. 'What's up?'

'I need some intel on a missing duckling. Have you seen her before?' Goldie asked as he held up the photo of Jess. Stumpy stared at the image, then shook his head.

'Have you seen anything unusual in the last couple of days? Any unfamiliar faces, strange things going on?' Manny interrupted.

Goldie shot a look at his new partner, but as Manny's question was his next question, he decided to wait for Stumpy's answer. Stumpy thought about it for a moment.

'You know what. Come to think of it, there was this bird. Last night, I've never seen anything like it. It was a giant bird, with a wingspan bigger… bigger than anything in this park!'

'What? Bigger than the King's?' Goldie asked.

'I think so,' Stumpy replied.

'It can't be,' said Goldie.

Goldie and Manny looked at each other as Stumpy continued talking.

'Put it this way, it's shadow covered my whole balcony. I wonder if that has something to do with it,' Stumpy finished.

'Bigger than anything in the park!' Goldie repeated.

'I'll put the word out and check in with you later,' Stumpy said before they said their goodbyes and left him to watch TV.

As Goldie and Manny walked away from Stumpy's tree, they walked around the lake. Goldie noticed a heron acting suspiciously. It was walking along the edge of the water with a wriggling bag in its hand. With every step it took, it looked over its shoulder nervously.

Goldie frowned. Instinct told him to find out what was in the bag. He ran after the heron, Manny followed.

'Freeze, Pond PD!' Goldie shouted.

Goldie ducked in front of the heron and pulled out his badge.

The heron attempted to fly away, but the wriggling bag was too heavy for its scrawny body and stopped the heron from taking flight.

The heron tossed the bag in the lake and tried to fly off again, but Goldie grabbed its wing and Manny did a Kung Fu kick to its stomach.

The two partners surrounded the heron.

'Get down on the ground and put your wings behind your back!' Goldie quacked, menacingly. The heron squawked as it dropped to the ground. Goldie stepped forwards and snapped some cuffs around its feet.

'Get the bag!' Goldie shouted to Manny.

Manny jumped into the water and disappeared. He emerged moments later, pulling the bag from the water.

Goldie carefully opened it; his heart was thumping inside his chest. He hoped that whatever was inside it was still alive.

He was relieved by the sight of a dozen tiny, peeping ducklings staring at him in terror.

'Holy mackerel!' Manny exclaimed.

Goldie looked for Jess but was unable to identify her amongst the ducklings.

'It's okay little ones, it's okay. We've got you now,' Goldie said reassuringly.

In the corner of his eye, he saw the heron trying to shuffle away. His eyes bulged with anger. He swept the heron's legs out from under him and stared down his bill at the criminal.

'You break the law in my park, and I'll put you behind chicken wire,' Goldie quacked menacingly.

He pulled the heron to its feet and frog-marched it towards Pond Police headquarters.

As they waddled, Goldie pulled some seeds from his pocket and gave them to Manny to share out amongst the ducklings.

When they reached the HQ, Mavis Scott, a hedgehog constable, took one look at the bedraggled ducklings and exclaimed, 'Oh my giddy goose, would you look at you! Let's get you cleaned up. I have a nice elderflower bubble bath ready for you!'

The ducklings chirped with excitement.

As the ducklings had their bath, Quackovitz, Goldie and Manny were summoned to see an even bigger cheese, the head of the Pond Police - Commander Cooper, a handsome fox.

'Get your uniforms dusted and your medals shined, you've been summoned to the Palace,' said Commander Cooper.

'We've done a count; there are over thirty younglings missing across the park. Ducklings, cygnets, baby rats, geese, fox cubs, froglets, hoglets, hatchlings, they're all *gone!* You've got an audience with the King and Queen in five minutes. And Quackovitz, don't put your beak in it this time!' he commanded.

## MISSING YOUNGLINGS

CYGNETS
Prince George

DUCKLINGS
Jess Green
Mina Behrozi
Cyra Behrozi
Sebastian Browne
Theodore Browne
Erlis Krasniqi
Melissa Krasniqi

FOX CUBS
Alaya Smith
Amber Deere
Charlie Glasscoe
Jamie Hayes
Vincent Nguyen

BABY MICE
Tia Purton
Maisie Sullivan

BABY BUNNIES
Chloe Ashby
Charlotte Nguyen
Ella Hayes
Harley Sullivan

HOGLETS
Corey Hayes
Paige Sumner

SQUIRRELS
Toby Sullivan
Tyler Sumner

HATCHLINGS
Kane Ashby
Kayleigh Millard

GOSLING
Harrison Millard

# MISSING

## HAVE YOU SEEN THIS DUCKLING?

**JESS GREEN**

IF YOU HAVE ANY INFORMATION PLEASE CALL

**THE POND POLICE**

# CHAPTER 6 - HERON ISLAND

Jess was scared and cold. She hugged her wings against her body as she and the other younglings were ushered through Heron Island.

It was a terrifying place, an impressive colony of fifty heron nests, each was high above the ground making them look like menacing towers.

Herons perched above the nests and stared down their blade-like bills watching for enemies and any unlucky prey who might've wandered the wrong way through the park. No one stepped foot there except the herons, no one *dared.*

Except today…

The younglings were led through a hole in the ground and into a cold, dark tunnel beneath the island. They walked through it shivering and shaking.

After what seemed like forever, they were led into a cave where they were left alone. They cried and peeped as a heron guard locked the door, plunging them into darkness.

Jess was tired and hungry. She knew the other younglings were terrified, yet their fear gave her courage. She had to be strong. But first, she had to find a way for them to work together.

She had to do what her mother told her before she jumped, she had to be "brave."

'Come on everyone,' peeped Jess. 'Stop crying. Gather together to keep warm. Come on, huddle up,' she insisted.

The younglings listened and huddled together. They took warmth in each other. Eventually the youngest ones, who'd been crying continuously, stopped and were silent.

'I know you're scared,' said Jess. 'I am too. But we have to work together if we want to get home.'

She stared at their faces with a look of determination.

On the other side of the island in a clearing, One-eyed Billy, the leader of the herons, sat on his make-shift throne of twigs and bones. He had a black eye patch over one eye, and he used his other eye to survey the families of his colony.

'Tomorrow, we take the first step in our park domination,' said One-eyed Billy.

A ROAR went up amongst the herons.

But as he spoke, a shadow passed over him. Billy's guards looked up as a giant bird dropped to the ground in front of them.

It was the biggest bird they'd ever seen - Hector.

In his talons, he held a smaller animal wrapped in leaves and branches, the animal was squawking and wriggling. No one could quite make out what it was.

The herons were in awe, they'd never seen a bird as fierce or frightening before.

Hector stalked over to Billy and stood over him.

'Move,' Hector demanded.

'Guards!' shouted Billy.

But the guards took one look at Hector's menacing face and fell back, more afraid of the giant eagle than of their heron leader.

Billy gulped.

'Who are you?' he squawked. He tried to hide the tremor in his voice, but Hector heard it and his eyes narrowed. He smiled, used to animals fearing him.

'I said. *Move*,' Hector repeated.

Billy lifted his scrawny feet and skinny legs and stepped off the throne. He watched as Hector dropped the squirming animal on the ground and took a seat on his throne.

But Billy's eyes widened in horror when he realised that the animal with Hector's claw clasped around its neck was none other than the young, swan prince, Prince George.

'What have you done?!' Billy screeched. He puffed out his chest. 'Are you mad? Who are you and what are you doing here?'

Hector sneered at the snivelling heron.

'I am your new King,' he said silkily. 'And by the way, tut, tut, tut. Ducklings… you're thinking *too* small. *I* will take control of this park, and *this* is how I will do it.'

He lifted his talons and pushed Prince George forwards. The cygnet tumbled across the ground, whimpering in terror.

'Please don't hurt me!' cried the frightened Prince.

'You can't do this!' Billy interrupted, he looked around him at his fellow herons. 'We won't let you!'

The herons looked at one another and whispered and murmured.

Screeeeeeeeech!

Hector dragged his talons across the ground, it was a horrible, deafening sound that made Billy's feathers stand on end.

'Open your little minds,' he said. 'With this Prince, I've given you the key. Everything you need to gain control of the kingdom. But it's *my* kingdom now and *I am* your leader.'

Billy thought about the eagle's suggestion.

Although Billy was afraid, he was also clever. He'd been trying to get control of the park for years. He couldn't stand the stuck-up King and Queen, and their brood of insufferable cygnets looking down their beaks at them all the time.

Perhaps Hector would make him his number two? Then he'd really have some power. Surely the eagle would one day get bored of the park and move on, then it would finally be HIS kingdom.

Billy made his decision, he fell to the ground and knelt in front of Hector.

'My King,' he clucked.

But on the other side of the park, another King was furious…

# CHAPTER 7 - SWAN PALACE

The Swan King and Queen sat on golden thrones in the throne room of the magnificent Swan Palace.

The Swan King was a large, white waterbird with a long S-shaped neck and an orange bill. Beside him perched his beautiful Queen. She was a smaller bird with a beautiful, sad face and pink-tinged feathers.

The Swan King stared down his bill at his Chief of Guards, an Egyptian goose.

'Who would dare steal my son! My Prince?!' he squawked as he looked to the goose for answers.

'We're looking into that right now, your Majesty,' replied the goose. 'We have scouts all over the park, on the ground and in the air.'

The Swan Palace had over one hundred Egyptian and Canadian geese to help keep the royal family safe. But the King and Queen knew that finding their son wouldn't be an easy task.

'The Pond Police will need help,' said the King.

'Yes. They rarely get involved in royal matters,' replied the Queen softly. But behind her softness was a steely determination to find her son.

'That's why I called in the M.I.DIVE, my dear,' said the Queen.

The King's eyes widened in surprise but before he could say anything, a bell rang out nearby to alert them to the arrival of the Pond Police.

'They should be here shortly,' said the Queen, who sat up straight on her throne and patted down her feathers.

They watched as the throne room doors opened and Goldie, Manny and Quackovitz waddled into the room. An Egyptian goose footman led them down the midnight blue walkway.

In all his time working for the Pond PD, Goldie had never been inside the palace. Over the years they'd offered to Knight him, but he always declined. He didn't like fuss, his only interest was doing his job and protecting the animals of the park.

Manny, however, looked around in awe, impressed by the magnificent room. There were paintings of swans on the

ceiling and columns of gold along the sides. In all his life, Manny had never been anywhere so grand.

When they reached the thrones, Quackovitz puffed out her chest and opened her beak, but the King raised his magnificent wings, silencing her.

'Now listen here, Quackovitz,' he drawled. 'I don't have time for your ruffled feathers. I'm concerned about the highly unusual number of missing younglings in *my* Kingdom!'

He sat back and wiped his forehead with his wing.

'And now my Prince, *my cygnet*. My son and heir is missing too. You can see how upset my Queen is. Tell me, who would dare kidnap him? The son of the rulers of the kingdom, the *biggest* birds in the park,' he finished, angrily.

Goldie saw the Queen wipe away a tear. He hoped his boss wouldn't put her webbed foot in it like she always did.

'Your Majesty,' Quackovitz bowed. 'We've searched the entire park from the tallest tree to the lowest parts of the lake and we've found nothing. But there've been reports of a large bird, your Majesty.'

Goldie closed his eyes.

For some reason, Quackovitz delighted in annoying the King, whenever they'd had dealings in the past. The King dismissed Quackovitz's ideas, and she didn't like it.

'What? Bigger than me?' demanded the King, unable to believe it. Quackovitz nodded.

The Queen placed her wing on the King's wing and gave him a look as if to say, '*be quiet.*'

The King sat back on his throne. His wings drooped and his eyes pierced Quackovitz's. Silence spread around the room, but it was soon broken by the sound of a bell ringing in the distance.

The throne room doors opened once more.

Goldie and Manny turned to see the Chief of Guards escorting five impressive birds of prey into the room. They were the elite M.I.DIVE team consisting of a Golden Eagle, a Peregrine Falcon, an American Bald Eagle, a Long-eared owl, and a Sparrowhawk.

'It's the M.I.DIVE. They only get involved in high profile cases,' said Manny.

'Shhh… I know,' whispered Goldie.

The birds of prey bowed when they reached the King and Queen.

Quackovitz eyed them warily. The King raised his wing. 'We've summoned you here to help me find my son,' he said.

But the Queen raised her own wing and interrupted the King. Her voice was soft and tired.

'Oh Bob, we haven't got all day,' she sweetly hissed, knowing full well her husband could honk on for hours…

The Swan Queen looked at the birds and ducks in front of them. 'Why don't you introduce yourselves?' she asked.

The largest bird, the Golden Eagle stepped forward and bowed.

'Ma'am, I'm James Beak, leader of the M.I.DIVE, this is Marcus Diaz, Peregrine Falcon,' said James.

Marcus, the Peregrine Falcon, had tapered wings and a slim, short tail. He had slate and blue-grey wings, black bars on his back, a white face with a black stripe on each cheek with large, dark eyes.

'To my right is Tom Cruz, an American Bald Eagle from the CIB,' said James.

Tom was a magnificent American Bald Eagle. He had a brown body and wings, a white head and tail, and a hooked yellow beak. His feet were also yellow with sharp, black talons.

Next, James pointed at Donnie Fostner, the Long-eared owl. Donnie had mottled orange-brown feathers, distinct white eyebrows, striking orange eyes and large ear tufts.

'And lastly, this is Jane Hart, Sparrowhawk,' finished James. Jane was a beautiful bird with brownish feathers. She had horizontal bars on her breast and grey wings. She bowed gracefully.

'Welcome,' said the King who pointed his wing at the Pond Police. 'This here is Chief Inspector Quackovitz and Detective Sergeant Goldie and Constable Manny from the Pond Police Department.'

Elite Birds of Prey
THE MI-DIVE
TOM CRUZ
Bald Eagle
JAMES BEAK
Golden Eagle
DONNIE FOSTNER
Long-eared Owl
JANE HART
Sparrowhawk
MARCUS DIAZ
Peregrine Falcon

The King continued…

'Sometimes crimes occur here in Kelsey Park. But it's always been managed. Balance has always been restored, that's nature. But what is happening now is unacceptable. I want my son and all the other younglings found and returned immediately. I want law and order restored to my kingdom. Bring them back!' he finished loudly.

The King and Queen retired leaving the Pond Police and M.I.DIVE to get acquainted. James Beak was the first to speak. He told them that Tom Cruz worked for the Central Intelligence Bureau for Birds, the CIB.

'Tom has a lot of knowledge of birds of prey from around the world, we thought he'd be useful. And Donny here specialises in the illegal eagle trade. He follows poachers who trade birds of prey around the world on Birdbook. We're not going to tell you what to do. We've heard some great things about you all so we're only here to advise and help you bring the younglings home.'

'Well, on behalf of the entire Pond PD, we want to thank you all for coming here. We're happy to have your help,' said Quackovitz who left Goldie in charge and retired.

Goldie, Manny and the M.I.DIVE stood outside the palace as the last of the blue and purple sky began to fade to black.

'Meet me here in the morning,' Goldie told them, 'I've got a plan.'

That evening, in the King and Queen's bed chamber, the King stood on the balcony and stared bleakly at the park. He was thinking about his son when the Queen joined him. She wrapped one of her wings around him.

'They'll find him, I just know it,' she said.

The King sighed. 'It's my fault, I pushed him away, I didn't appreciate or spend enough time with him. All I did was hiss at him; "do this, don't do that." I just wanted to help him grow.'

'Listen to me,' said the Queen, she turned his face to meet hers with her wing. 'You're a wonderful father and King. It wasn't easy for you, and it won't be easy for George. But he loves you. Wherever he is, he knows you're doing everything you can to find him.'

A few metres away, beneath Heron Island, Prince George lay in a cold dark cave alone, shivering and shaking. Every so

often, a heron guard came to check on him to give him food and water, but the prince was too frightened to eat or drink.

A short while later, Hector sent a guard to move the prince to the same cave as the other younglings. The prince was no good to him dead - perhaps he would eat with the others.

# CHAPTER 8 - FLY BY

The next morning, Goldie, Stumpy and the M.I.DIVE stood outside Stumpy's tree.

The birds of prey were too big to fit inside.

'Can you fly past so Stumpy can compare your size to the other bird?' Goldie asked.

'A fly-by!' Marcus squawked, excitedly.

Goldie wanted to see if the bird Stumpy had seen was bigger or smaller than the M.I. DIVE team. Then they might have a clue as to what kind of bird it was.

Marcus jumped up and puffed out his chest.

Jane Hart rolled her eyes at Marcus.

'Fly past slowly, Marcus,' she ordered.

Donnie stood beside Jane and shook his head with annoyance, his ear tufts shaking all over the place.

'Stop mucking around and fly by properly!' he hooted at Marcus, who was now on the grass puffing out his grey chest with importance.

'We don't have time for all his puffing and preening!' Donnie said to Jane with a slight wink of his eye, Jane laughed.

Goldie, Stumpy, Manny and Grandad stood outside on the balcony as the team took it in turns to fly past the tree.

'They're right! Don't fly too fast, Marcus! They won't see you!' James shouted.

But Marcus had already taken off, he flew up high then dived down through the air and shot past the treehouse at over two-hundred miles per hour.

'Wow!' exclaimed Manny as a gust of wind from Marcus's tailwind ruffled his feathers.

Goldie, Stumpy and Grandad were impressed.

***Peregrine Falcons are the fastest birds in the world. When in a dive, they can reach speeds of over two-hundred and twenty miles per hour.***

Marcus was like lightning. He passed them in the blink of an eye and was so fast that they couldn't see him.

Jane shook her head. 'He never listens,' she said ruefully. James nodded in agreement.

'Go again!' James shouted to Marcus. 'Slowly!'

This time Marcus flew by much slower, but he was still fast. Stumpy stared up at Marcus hard, then shook his head. 'The other bird was bigger,' he said.

The last one to fly past was James, the largest bird on the team, but even he was too small.

Stumpy shook his head again. 'Nope, it was bigger than all of you.'

Tom Cruz, who was perched on a branch, spun upside down and stared at Stumpy. 'Did you notice anything else about the bird, even the slightest detail could help us,' Tom said.

'I think it had a kind of crest on its head, a few feathers stuck up, like a turkey,' said Stumpy.

'Hmmm...' Tom was silent for a moment. 'The bird I think you're talking about sounds like a Harpy Eagle.'

Goldie's eyes widened; he'd seen a Duck Attenborough program on Harpy eagles a few years ago. A shiver flew down his spine.

Tom continued. 'They're one of the biggest birds in the world and one of the most dangerous. A report came into the CIB a few weeks back that there was a missing Harpy from Brazil somewhere in Europe, but I had no idea it'd be here.' He looked at Goldie. 'This is trouble.'

'Sounds like our eagle,' said James.

'A bird that big can't just disappear,' said Goldie. 'Someone must've seen it. We need to find out where it's hiding.'

'We'll search the tallest trees, but I have a feeling this bird is clever. He must've found a way to conceal himself really well,' said James, with a shake of his feathers.

For the rest of the day, half the team flew around the park in circle formation, searching the perimeter while Manny and Marcus went off to investigate leads. They all met back at the palace grounds that evening.

Goldie addressed the team. 'You must be tired. There are rooms prepared for you at the Palace. Why don't you rest up and we'll re-group in the morning.'

'Manny, in the morning go with Marcus and keep sweating the animals out, chase down leads before we meet. We've got to put the pressure on. Get them quacking,' Goldie said.

Manny nodded.

'We'll take it in turns to sleep, while two of us fly around the perimeter. We'll make sure nothing goes out and nothing comes in,' James said.

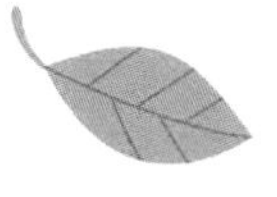

But nothing happened, the skies were empty, and the park was quiet except for Puddletown, the bustling city in the heart of the park which was always noisy.

On their way home, Goldie and Manny waddled down the cobbled streets which were abuzz with animals doing their shopping. Goldie popped inside Puddlestone's Bookshop to buy a book on Harpy Eagles.

Waitrosie
PuddLestone's
BOOK SHOP
Giggling Squid
PUDDLETOWN
STARDUCKS
FEATHERED FRIENDS
BLOSSOM
Bakery

‘I’ll go through it tonight and see what I can find out about the eagle,’ Goldie said.

‘Looks like you have an exciting night ahead of you,’ Manny chuckled.

‘Someone’s got to do it,’ Goldie replied, ruefully. ‘What are you doing tonight?’

‘Watching “Bad Birds,”’ said Manny in excitement. ‘It’s an awesome cop film.’

Goldie guffawed. ‘Never heard of it. If you want to watch a *real* cop film watch “Lethal Talon”,’ he said. Manny said goodnight and waddled home.

As Goldie walked past the Feathered Friends pub he spotted Patrick Green. Patrick was staring into a full pint of snail ale, sadly. Goldie walked over to him, and Patrick looked up.

‘Any news?’ he asked hopefully.

Goldie shook his head and put his wing on the Mandarin Duck’s shoulder.

'We have a great team looking for Jess, as soon as I find anything out, you and Anne will be the first to know,' said Goldie.

Patrick managed a slight smile.

'Thank you,' he said as he pushed the glass away without drinking it.

'I can't face going home, all Anne and the young'un's do is cry. I don't know what to say to them,' he said, hopelessly.

Goldie patted his friend's shoulder. He knew that no words of reassurance would comfort him in a terrible situation like this.

# CHAPTER 9 - THE CAVES

On Heron Island, the herons were having trouble managing the younglings, and Jess kept asking questions and demanding seeds and water for them.

News of her behaviour soon reached Hector. 'Bring her to me,' he commanded. 'I could do with a succulent snack,' he said as he licked his lips in anticipation.

Two heron guards brought wriggling Jess to Hector's cave.

'This one won't stop quacking. Think she's trying to lead them,' said one of the guards.

'Yeah, she's a real busy body,' squawked the other. He pushed Jess towards Hector. The little duckling wobbled but stood up tall as she stared at the huge eagle.

'I'm not afraid of you,' said Jess defiantly.

'You should be!' barked one of the guards. 'Let me eat her, Hector!' 'No,' said Hector, firmly. 'No one gets eaten, yet...'

He stared down at the little yellow and brown smudge.

'What's to be afraid of here?' Hector drawled, 'We're all friends…' he said, as he came closer to her and opened his wings. They were like a huge curtain surrounding Jess.

Jess gulped and shrank down a bit.

'What's your name, Little Wing?' asked Hector.

'I… I… I don't talk to strangers,' Jess stuttered stubbornly.

'Suit yourself, Little Wing,' Hector said with a smile.

Jess's feathers ruffled in anger at the name.

'It's Jess,' she said, with a scowl. 'I want to go home!' she demanded.

Hector threw back his head and laughed. It was a loud bellow like the clap of thunder as it rumbles through the clouds.

'This is your home now, Little Wing,' he said silkily.

'No, it's *not*!' Jess argued.

Hector had had enough of the drama. His stomach rumbled and he decided to eat the annoying duckling. He opened his beak and bent down…

Jess's eyes widened in horror, and she stepped back.

'How would *you* feel if someone took you away from your home? Your family?' she said, as tears fell down her cheeks.

Hector knew what *that* felt like.

He closed his beak with a snap. Shame had made him stop from eating her.

His eyes narrowed as he looked at the duckling, she really was tiny. He could squash her with the tip of one of his talons. But he admired her nerve for such a small thing.

Hector sighed.

'I *was* taken from *my* home. From my mate and our chicks. So, I'm trying to create a *new* life for myself, right here, Little Wing, until I can find my way home,' he finished quietly.

For a few minutes, Hector told Jess about where he came from. Her eyes widened when he described Amazonia. Jess wished she could see it for herself. She felt sorry for Hector and felt his sadness.

But Hector saw her sad, little eyes and knew he'd revealed too much. The guards were looking at him, probably thinking he'd gone soft. He had no idea *why* he'd revealed so much to the duckling and began to regret it.

'Let us go home!!' shouted Jess with as much courage as she could muster.

Hector bent down. His wings drew even closer around her, and she shrank back again in terror.

'If only it were that simple. Let me tell you a secret. This is *my* kingdom now. *I'm* its ruler. So, you might want to do as you're told or you'll never see your family again.'

Jess's beak quivered. Tears formed in her eyes, and she peeped and chirped with anger and sadness.

Hector shook his head and stepped back. For a moment, he was ashamed of his actions and he didn't like the feeling.

‘Take her away now!’ he commanded the guards.

When the duckling was gone, Hector stared at the walls. It was a dull, dark place. His thoughts returned to his home, and his family. Without him, they were all alone. He hoped his chicks had courage like Jess.

# CHAPTER 10 - EAGLE EYES

While Goldie and Manny were out investigating leads, the M.I.DIVE soared through the sky. Using their long-distance vision, they searched the park for the younglings.

The eagles had the best sight of all the team.

***An eagle can see eight times as far as humans and can spot a rabbit from a distance of two miles.***

The team circled Heron Island several times but could only see the herons going about their usual business.

Beneath the island, One-eyed Billy paced around his cave. He ignored the sounds of the younglings chirping and peeping in the next cave.

As he paced, two of his guards reported to him that the M.I.DIVE were searching the skies above the island.

Billy was scared, he knew that once the M.I.DIVE were involved things could get tricky.

'They solve every case!' said one of the guards. 'They'll find the cave,' said the other.

'Maybe this wasn't such a good idea after all,' Billy replied. 'Hector's gone too far by taking the prince.'

But Billy was interrupted by the sound of a claw scraping across the cave wall. He closed his eyes, anticipating Hector bearing down on him.

In one swoop, Hector's claw clamped around Billy's neck. He raised the heron off the ground as if he weighed nothing more than a feather.

Hector turned his head to the side as he stared into the heron's terrified eye.

'You were saying…' Hector prompted.

Billy tried to speak but only a few squawks came out because of Hector's tight grip.

'I'll show you ALL how a kingdom is ruled,' Hector said, as he let go of Billy, who fell to the ground.

Hector stormed out of the cave and launched himself into the sky. He flew over the lake and the water rippled beneath him, like the sea before a storm.

He flew high then dived down low and into the royal kingdom.

The kingdom was abuzz with activity, there were geese patrolling the borders and skies. When the soldiers saw Hector flying towards them, they flew at him in attack formation, but he just breezed through them, sending them tumbling through the air and into the water with a splash.

A young swan shrank in terror when Hector flew over her. 'Oh, my goodness!' she squawked.

Gail Feathers, a female wood duck reporter from the Bird Gazette stood outside the palace with her camera crew. She was in the middle of recording an update on the missing prince and younglings.

Gail was a sharp reporter and a beautiful duck, but her smart face was overshadowed by a flashy beak and massive mane of enhanced feathers.

'There've been sightings of a big bird in Kelsey Park. Eye-witnesses don't know what type of bird it is but...' Gail stopped in mid-sentence when Hector flew over her.

'OH MY FEATHERS! There it is! There's the bird! Oh, what a bird! It looks like an eagle, but no eagle I've ever seen!' she cried in bewilderment.

Hector flew past Gail and down into the courtyard of the palace. He knew that everyone in the kingdom had seen him, he sensed their fear with triumph as he flew towards the palace gates.

Gail noticed her cameraduck's beak was wide open. She stopped and spun around as Hector flew over her.

'KEEP UP WITH ME!' Gail shouted at her cameraduck.

Gail flew after Hector and towards the palace as the animals walking around the kingdom fled in terror. As the terrifying bird descended upon the palace, Hector's shadow seemed to block out the sun.

The Egyptian and Canadian geese guards pulled on their silver armour, ready for battle as the King flew out of the palace with a group of guards behind him.

Gail settled her feathers as her cameraduck began filming.

'This is Gail Feathers from BIRD-MORNING coming to you live with exclusive footage of the bird who has been terrorising the park. There it is! There's the bird! And, what a bird. It's an eagle, but no eagle I've ever seen before!'

The King met Hector in the middle of the courtyard just as Goldie, Manny and Marcus arrived. None of the birds had ever seen an eagle like him before. Hector could see in the King's eyes that he knew it too - they were no match for him.

'Go get James and Tom,' Goldie shouted to Marcus who took off into the sky in search of his teammates.

Hector watched the interaction between Goldie and Marcus, his eyes narrowed as he stared at Goldie.

'What do you want, eagle!' shouted the King. Hector turned. He and the King glared at one another.

'I'm not here to fight you, old bird,' said Hector, arrogantly. 'Give me back my son!' yelled the King.

'I'm here to tell you how it's going to go. I have your son, your prince, and all the other younglings in the park,' Hector gloated.

The geese guards closed in on him, but Hector didn't look concerned. He ignored them as if they were nothing. Goldie and Manny came up and stood behind the King, to offer support.

'If these elite birds of prey team don't leave, and you don't follow *my* rules, you'll never see *any* of them again!' Hector finished.

'You have to earn a kingdom, eagle,' said the King.

'I'm not your average bird,' Hector drawled. 'If I want something, I take it. That's what we Harpys do.'

He lifted a foot and licked his talons while the outraged King's eyes bulged.

'I won't have it!' he shouted.

'*You* won't have what?' Hector asked in annoyance.

Hector had had enough. He flew at the King and caught him around the neck with his claw. His three huge talons dug into the swan's white feathers. The King was still and silent.

'This is *my* kingdom now,' Hector snarled.

The Queen appeared and flew out of the palace to her husband's aid. 'Get away you villain!' she hissed.

Hector let go of the King, who fell to the ground, humiliated in front of the entire palace. He turned to the Queen.

'Maybe you can talk some sense into him,' Hector said, with a raised eyebrow.

He turned around to see Goldie and Manny storming towards him with several birds of prey behind them.

With all the guards and police, Hector knew he was outnumbered. But he waited for Goldie and Manny to get close to him so they could see his size.

Goldie and Manny stopped in their tracks and helped the King stand up again. Hector barely gave them a glance.

'As I said before, you can have your son back when I have my kingdom,' Hector said smoothly as the group were almost upon him.

'I'll be back in three days with your *prince*, and I will claim my kingdom,' Hector said, before he took a run and shot off into the sky, his huge wings spread out wide.

As Hector flew away, the animals on the ground stared in terror.

'I've never seen a bird like that! He's a monster!' Manny exclaimed.

Goldie nodded. 'How did he get in here? We need to secure the palace.'

For the next day, the Pond Police and M.I.DIVE stood guard on the palace. Nobody wanted to leave their homes. Animals stayed inside; foxes wouldn't let their cubs out of their dens, birds and ducks wouldn't let their younglings out of their nests, everyone feared the big, bad eagle.

Goldie and Manny gathered Stumpy and the M.I.DIVE together.

'We have to find him now,' Goldie said. 'I've done some research and I think he might be somewhere on Heron Island.'

Quackovitz's eyes lit up. 'Yes, the herons have been unusually quiet. I bet they're working with the eagle.'

Goldie nodded.

'We need to get on the island and see if the younglings are there. All of us birds are too big, we need someone small and stealthy to sneak on there.' He looked at Stumpy. 'Will you help us?'

'Of course,' said Stumpy. 'But give me a few minutes, I need to check in with some animals, and then I'll be ready.'

While they waited, Goldie, Manny and the M.I.DIVE discussed their next moves.

James perched on a branch. 'This eagle is crafty,' he sighed.

'We need to make a trap. Let's lure him in and catch him once and for all,' Goldie suggested.

He made a circular motion on the ground with his webbed foot, all the team members gathered in close whilst Goldie made a map of the park with his foot.

'Oh, come on! Let's not get bogged down by all the details,' Marcus interrupted, impatiently.

'Let's just get him!' he said, as he raised his wings with excitement.

James and Tom smiled and shook their heads.

'Slow down, young peregrine,' said Goldie. 'It's patience and details that help you win a battle. We have to trick him into flying into the trap.'

'He's our kind, sir,' Marcus insisted. 'We'll take him down!'

'Hogswash!' said Goldie, with a chuckle. But he soon turned serious. 'In this park, everyone is our kind, Marcus. We're here to protect ALL animals. From the toad to the heron, to the snail and the fox.'

Marcus thought about Goldie's words then nodded. His impatience always got the better of him, but he knew that the golden duck was right.

They spent the rest of the afternoon building the trap between two tall trees. They built a vast web of chicken wire that stretched from tree to tree like a snare.

'We'll have to catch him at night, or he'll see it. In the dark it's harder to see unless you know it's there,' James said as they finished up.

That night, the ducks and the M.I.DIVE stood beneath a tree as they surveyed Heron Island. It was still and silent until a nearby rustle alerted them. Tom Cruz turned, talons at the ready, but it was only Stumpy returning to give them an update.

'I heard through the grapevine that there's a cave beneath the island. If the younglings are anywhere, that's where they'll be,' he reported.

'Do you think they're still alive?' Stumpy asked Goldie.

Goldie nodded. 'They're his bargaining chip. He won't give it away. But I think I should come with you, Stumpy,' Goldie suggested.

Stumpy shook his head.

'You're too big, we'll get caught. I can do this,' he insisted.

'Okay, but just be careful,' Goldie replied. 'Look what happened on your last mission.'

Stumpy laughed. 'You all think losing half my tail was a disadvantage. But believe me, it made me quicker!' Stumpy said with a wink.

James shook Stumpy's paw. 'You're one brave squirrel. If you find the younglings don't try and rescue them alone though, let us know where they are, and we'll assist you.'

Stumpy nodded as he pulled off his rucksack and emptied the contents onto the ground. Inside it was his ninja costume; a head-to-toe outfit he'd fashioned out of a pair of old human socks he'd found in one of the park bins.

The others turned around as Stumpy pulled on the costume. When he was dressed, he peered through the bushes. He felt comfort knowing the others were behind him.

The park was silent except for the faint rustling of trees. But the wind had picked up and it felt like a storm was coming. A drop of rain landed on Goldie's beak.

He looked across at Stumpy.

'Better now than never,' suggested Goldie.

Stumpy nodded and took a deep breath. He leapt onto the nearest tree and silently swung from branch to branch, tree to tree. He was like a flying squirrel as he made his way towards the creepy island.

'Think it's time we put on the war paint,' said Jane.

Goldie and the M.I.DIVE covered themselves in mud from the edges of the lake, while Jane drew thick lines of mud under Goldie, Manny and the M.I.DIVE's eyes, when she had finished she stepped back to admire her handiwork.

When their camouflage was complete, They perched on the top of a tall tree. Its branches swayed and bits of twigs broke off as the wind and rain grew stronger and turned into a storm.

'Has anyone see Hector?' Goldie shouted above the noise.

Marcus had the best eyesight of the team, so he scanned the park.

'Nope,' he said, disappointed.

Manny looked at Goldie with concern. 'It's gonna be a big storm. This mission isn't looking possible right now,' he said with worry etched across his face.

Goldie shook his head. 'Not for our Stumpy,' he said with a smile. But a gust of wind blew his feathers and he looked up at the sky.

'And you're right, there is a storm coming,' he said loudly, so all the other birds could hear. 'The eagle has to be stopped… and we're going to do it.'

Goldie turned and looked across the water. He stared at the banks of Heron Island while he waited for Stumpy's return and hopefully some good news.

# CHAPTER 11 - STUMPY'S MISSION

Stumpy reached Heron Island in no time. He leapt through bushes and scurried up and down trees. Because of his size and agility, he was able to slip by unnoticed so he managed to avoid being seen by the heron guards stationed around the perimeter.

The rain was pouring now. He was thankful for it as it provided cover and it meant that some of the herons went inside their nests to avoid the bad weather. On the left side of the island, he found a small cave entrance. He crept into it and found himself inside a narrow tunnel.

As he walked down the tunnel, he noticed a flash of colour on the ground. He reached down and picked up a yellow and brown feather. He continued walking and every so often he found another feather, then another. *Someone's left a trail!*

Stumpy was hopeful as he followed the crumbs, until finally, he found a small cave with a metal door. A heron guard was standing outside the cave. Luckily, the guard was asleep.

Using his ninja skills, Stumpy leapt silently across the ground and crept behind the sleeping heron. He turned and used the pointy tip of his tail stump to pick the lock.

Stumpy slid inside the door and silently closed it behind him. The cave appeared to be empty. He took out an acorn lantern from his pocket and lit it. A second later, the cave was flooded with a warm glow.

There were ducklings, baby squirrels, mice and rabbits, fox cubs, hoglets, hatchlings, tiny birds, and a gosling.

A brazen little brown and yellow face stepped towards Stumpy and held up her wings, ready to fight.

'Who are you?' demanded Jess. Stumpy noticed that some of her feathers were missing.

'Slow down, little duckling. I'm here to help! These must be yours,' Stumpy said as he held out the feathers.

The younglings stared at him hopefully.

Stumpy gave the acorn lantern to Jess. 'Here, take it.'

'I'm Stumpy. I'm with the Pond Police and M.I.DIVE. They sent me to find you. There's too many guards out there so I can only take one of you with me,' he said apologetically.

'Oh! Thank goodness, we're saved!' came the terrified voice of Prince George, who came to see what was going on. But his voice fell when he saw Stumpy.

'One squirrel against *all* those herons?!' he said in fright.

'I don't see any of your palace guards anywhere!' said a fox cub. 'M.I.DIVE eagles?' said an excited little hatchling.

Stumpy nodded. 'And the palace guards!' he said, with a smile. There were peeps and chirps all around him.

'Shhhhhh!' Stumpy said. 'You have to be quiet.'

'My feet are wet,' complained a hoglet. Jess went over to her and noticed a puddle of water that hadn't been there earlier.

'Maybe there's a leak,' she suggested.

Stumpy ran to the back of the cave to investigate. Rainwater was pouring in through a crack and was rising fast. Soon the crack grew to a large hole.

'Listen everyone, there's a storm outside and it's caused a leak in the cave. I don't want to scare you, but we have to leave!'

'This mission is impossible!' exclaimed Prince George, witha shake of his terrified head.

Stumpy turned. 'Not for me it isn't.'

The others had told Stumpy to wait to evacuate the younglings, but with the water rising so fast he knew he had to get them out through the tunnels now.

On the other side of the lake, Goldie was getting anxious. The rain poured down and tree branches creaked and cracked in the howling wind. Animals across the park battened down their hatches, too afraid to leave their homes.

'Something's gone wrong,' Goldie said to the others. 'Stumpy should be back by now.'

James approached Goldie. 'We're going to need more air support.' He turned to Marcus. 'Marcus fly back to Headquarters and alert them,' he finished.

Marcus, eager to be of use, took a running leap into the sky and was gone before Goldie could blink.

Goldie addressed the team. 'We have to get over there now. Let's swim under the water and come up on the edge of the bank beneath that sunken log.'

James nodded. 'We'll fly over.'

Back on Heron Island, Stumpy, Prince George and Jess led the younglings through the tunnels. The water rose rapidly behind them.

The prince was starting to feel useful and a little less scared, but every little sound set his nerves on edge, and he was worried that they'd get caught.

'Come along now everyone,' urged Stumpy. He wanted them out before the tunnels were completely submerged. But they soon heard guards running after them, so Stumpy pulled some pinecones from his pocket and attached them to his tail.

'STUMPY!' shouted Jess as the guards approached.

One of the guards ran at Stumpy who turned and did a Kung Fu kick to its stomach. He then spun around knocking over two more guards with his tail-cones.

He waited for more guards to arrive but there were none.

The younglings were scared but Jess encouraged them to keep moving. Soon they all exited the cave into the storm.

As they ran towards the water, Jess and the younglings held on tight to one another so they wouldn't be blown away by the gale-force winds.

A Pond Police frog was waiting for them by the lake.

'Goldie sent me!' she shouted above the noise. Her eyes widened when she saw the younglings tumble out of the cave.

'What are *they* doing here?' she shouted.

'I had to get them out!' Stumpy shouted back. 'The caves were flooding!' he explained. 'We need to get across the lake, *now!*'

A few miles away, Marcus reached the M.I.DIVE headquarters in London. It was inside a big tree in Hyde Park.

'I can't hang around, Sir,' he frantically told his supervisor, Commander Snarl. 'My friends are in trouble!'

Commander Snarl was a white-tailed eagle - the largest bird of prey in the United Kingdom. He was an impressive bird with brown body feathers and snow-white tail feathers.

'A Harpy Eagle, in England…' said Commander Snarl, as he stared out the window at the gloomy sky and shook his head.

'It's unheard of… but don't worry help is on the way. We'll send down a team to help capture him. You might want to take the flight path over Brixton on your way back, it'll be smoother.'

'Will do, sir,' said Marcus with a nod. Commander Snarl opened the window.

'Good luck, Agent Diaz,' he said as he watched Marcus fly out into the clouds.

Back on Heron Island, Stumpy was afraid that the smallest younglings wouldn't make the journey.

But out of the darkness, Goldie and the others appeared from inside some trees and bushes, running and flying towards them.

Stumpy stopped and breathed a sigh of relief.

The younglings peeped and chirped with excitement.

'Come on! Let's go!' Goldie shouted.

'Where are the herons?' asked Manny.

'I dealt with some of them, but more will come, so we have to be quick,' Stumpy said, urgently.

Goldie and the M.I.DIVE found a floating log and led the younglings onto it, Prince George was one of the first to hurry on. But there wasn't enough room for Jess, so Goldie placed her on his back.

'You can sit next to Stumpy,' he said.

Goldie looked at James and Tom. 'We need to hurry, it's only a matter of time before they alert Hector. I'm surprised he doesn't already know we're here.'

As they crossed the lake, Jess was excited, it was the first time she'd been in the water. She was also excited to be reunited with her family.

They swam over to the log and helped to push it across to the other side of the lake.

A few miles away, a rumble of thunder echoed across the sky as Marcus flew back from London.

Some birds don't like storms, but Marcus loved the thrill of danger. He'd free-fall and dive amongst the clouds, dodging the lightning. But this time he was worried about his friends, there was no time for games, and he flew faster than the wind.

When the rooftops of Beckenham became visible, Marcus dived down in the direction of the park. As he plunged, he tucked in his wings, which increased his speed and he hit over two-hundred and forty miles per hour. But he couldn't maintain the speed for long, so he slowed down when he reached the entrance to the park.

An army of herons flew beneath Marcus. The birds flew with their necks tucked against their bodies, in an "S" shape. Marcus followed them towards Heron Island.

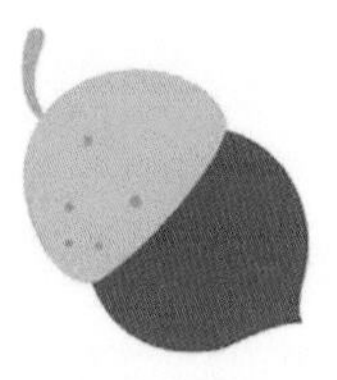

# CHAPTER 12 - HECTOR "THE HORRID"

One-eyed Billy had just finished cleaning fish slime off his chest when his guards burst into his cave and informed him that the younglings had been taken.

He was reluctant to tell Hector the bad news.

'This has gone too far,' Billy cried. 'This is crazy. They'll *all* be after us now. This isn't the way we work.' He sighed. 'We're usually just waiting in the shallows.'

His heron guards nodded in agreement.

'It's my fault, we should've stuck to how things were. The normal way; taking a few younglings every week.'

'We were only doing what the eagle made us do!' one of the guards said, to show solidarity. 'No one likes him, Billy. The other guards are even calling him "Hector the Horrid", he's awful.'

Billy nodded then sighed. 'Come on, I'd better tell him.'

Of course, Hector was furious when he heard the news that Goldie and the other birds had saved the younglings.

Billy's complaining only enraged him further.

'We didn't expect it to get this serious, Hector,' snivelled Billy. 'Things are getting out of hand. Detective Goldie's working with the M.I.DIVE and they've been watching the island. Now they've taken back what we took - and if the M.I.DIVE are involved - we're in real danger.'

Hector was silent for a long moment then he hit the wall with his wing.

'That duck keeps interfering with my plans!' he squawked.

'He's the top detective in the park,' said Billy.

'Hector, you're taking us down the wrong path. If we follow you any longer, we could be banished from the park forever and I'm sorry, but there's *no* other place I'd rather call home,' Billy said, quietly.

'What is all this snivelling and whining?' screeched Hector, who flew at Billy and swiped his wing, sending the heron flying.

'How dare you question me!!' he bellowed.

'Who do you think you are? *I am your King*, heron!'

But Billy stood up tall and proud, he looked Hector in the eye with his one good eye. '*Half* my herons will follow me, Hector. The *other* half are yours. But *we* will follow you no more.'

A few of Billy's brave guards came forward slowly and pulled him back to safety, they surrounded him like a shield.

Hector's eyes narrowed. 'I don't need *you* anyway!' he said, his eyes flashing. 'I'll deal with this myself, and I'm going to put an end to that interfering duck detective. Now, come with me!' he said as he glared at the rest of the guards.

A dozen herons nervously stepped forwards to join Hector's ranks, while Billy and his own small team cowered.

Hector gave Billy one last menacing stare before he and his heron guards left the cave and went into the storm.

'Follow me!' Hector ordered the guards, his eyes red with fury. He shot up into the air a hundred feet and spun around.

As he moved his feathers and wings spun around with him in a swirling motion. He stopped mid-air and hovered above the trees as the wind crashed against him and the rain splattered off his body.

Hector searched for his prey. It took him only seconds to spot Goldie and the others. He spun in their direction.

'This way!' he shouted to the guards.

When the log reached the edge of the lake, Goldie, Stumpy and Jess were only seconds behind it. Some of the parents had arrived in a hurry when they learnt of the rescue mission and there was a commotion as they searched for their young amongst the many faces.

But a few minutes later, a piercing squawk echoed across the sky above them.

Goldie turned. A movement to the east alerted him to Hector and the herons who were streaking towards him.

Stumpy and Jess looked behind them too. 'It's the eagle!' shouted Stumpy.

'Quick, quick! They're coming!' shouted Jess.

Goldie swam as fast as he could until he reached the bank.

'Get out of here!' Goldie shouted to Stumpy and Jess, who jumped off his back and ran to safety.

Jess saw the group of parents huddled by the side of the lake. She knew that somewhere amongst them her parents would be waiting, but she wanted to see what would happen with Goldie and Hector.

'Come on let's follow them!' Jess said to a startled Prince George who was standing nearby waiting for the palace guards.

Prince George looked up as Hector disappeared out of sight. He was starting to feel more confident; spending time with Jess had influenced him to be more courageous and braver. So instead of finding his family, he followed Jess.

Cries went up all around as Hector and the herons neared the animals on the shoreline.

The M.I.DIVE sprang into action and fought them. They tumbled around the sky swiping and clawing each other, spinning and diving, trying to evade one another.

Hector shot away from the M.I.DIVE and after Goldie. He swooped down towards him.

'I'm going to destroy you!' he shouted.

Goldie turned around and saw Hector seconds behind him. Now was the perfect time for him to put his plan into motion. He took a running leap into the sky and flew through the park with Hector right behind him.

Unlike Hector, Goldie was small and agile, and most importantly, Hector didn't know the park like Goldie did.

Goldie flew through bushes and around trees. He sent the eagle on a merry goose chase, making him fly around in circles, backwards and forwards, and up and down.

They flew back over the lake and around the perimeter. They flew over Puddletown where they bumped into the side of the Blossom Bakery and some tiles fell off the roof of the pub. A hedgehog walking on the street below got the fright of his life as a tile narrowly missed his head.

Twice, Hector almost swiped Goldie with his talons, but each time he got close, Goldie spun away at the last second and escaped him.

Goldie flipped sideways leaving Hector to fly into a tree and fall to the ground. Hector was getting more furious by the second. When he got up, he clenched his talons, but Goldie just flew around the tree, taunting him and flapping his wings at Hector. Hector flew up to Goldie and continued to chase him around the park.

Behind them, James, Tom, Donnie and Jane were still fighting off the other herons. But after they defeated each heron, another would appear, then another, it was like a never-ending barrage of herons.

Tom had had enough and dived towards the surface of the lake, using his outstretched talons he sprayed the water over a group of herons who fell into the lake.

Marcus arrived and flew over to James. 'Help… is on the… way,' he said, out of breath.

They both looked over and saw Goldie being chased by Hector.

'Come with me, we've got to help Goldie!' shouted James. 'Hector will kill him!'

James and Marcus flew after Hector. When they found him, he had Goldie pinned up against the top of a tree with his talons wrapped around his neck.

'You've meddled in my business too long, duck,' Hector snarled.

He was just about to use his lethal talon, but then he hesitated. This gave James some time to fly into him making him lose his balance and crash to the ground.

When he'd recomposed himself, Hector flew up at James and they began to battle each other.

In mid-air, Hector and James thrashed their wings and talons trying to tear each other apart. Every so often, Marcus flew in-between them to give Hector a quick swipe.

But Hector also knew some tricks. He used his talon to flick bark from the side of a tree into James's eyes, temporarily blinding him while he gave the golden eagle a good swipe with his talon.

Marcus flew at Hector.

'That was a cheap shot! See if you can catch *me*, eagle!' Marcus shouted as he turned and dashed away through the sky.

Hector took the bait and chased after Marcus. Marcus led Hector towards the trap and straight into the flight path of

Goldie who'd flown ahead of them.

Goldie stood on the top of a tree just in front of the trap, looking confident and self-assured. When Hector saw him, his eyes bulged, he flew away from Marcus and after Goldie. He relentlessly closed in on his prey.

Goldie sensed that Hector was seconds away.

He turned and his eyes locked onto the incredible eagle that was just about to kill him.

Goldie knew that if Hector didn't fly into the trap now, he never would, so he flew faster than he'd ever flown before.

Hector focused on Goldie with tunnel vision and unknowingly flew towards the two trees where the trap was suspended in mid-air.

As Hector closed in on Goldie, he spread his wings out wide to slow his descent. He reached his talons forward as he would when catching prey.

A sense of triumph ran through him. But just as he reached Goldie's tail feathers, the golden duck shot under the trap leaving Hector to fly straight into it.

The chicken wire wrapped around Hector and tangled his wings up. Hector's body curled into a ball. The momentum of his speed carried him through the chicken wire until he was completely entangled in it and couldn't move.

Hector crashed to the ground.

He winced in pain, then everything went black.

The other birds came together and surrounded Hector, who lay motionless on the ground.

'Is he dead?' asked Marcus.

Goldie pushed Hector's body with his foot. He noticed a few drops of blood at the side of the eagle's mouth.

'Looks like it,' said Stumpy who'd come to join them. He was with Chief Inspector Quackovitz and Commander Snarl, who'd just arrived with a team of a dozen birds of prey.

Commander Snarl took charge. 'Let's leave him here for the night,' he said. 'He's going nowhere. We can come back in the morning and decide what to do with him.'

Quackovitz nodded. 'If he's still alive, we'll put him in a cell and see what the King wants to do with him.'

Commander Snarl nodded and ordered his other birds to round up all the herons.

When the commotion had died down, Goldie looked up at the sky, the rain and wind had stopped, and the storm was now over. Goldie breathed a sigh of relief.

Celebrations took place across the park when the animals learnt that Hector had been caught.

When word of his capture reached Anne and Patrick, they jumped with excitement. They were still standing amongst the group of parents waiting to be reunited with their younglings.

But there were fewer and fewer younglings left as their parents had now come to take them home. Patrick and Anne soon realised that Jess wasn't amongst them, and a wave of fear and terror ran through them.

# CHAPTER 13 - LITTLE WING

Jess and Prince George came out from behind some mushrooms where they'd been secretly hiding. Everyone had gone and it was just them and the eagle.

'What a horrid eagle. Looks like he's dead. Serves him right,' said Prince George. 'Come on, let's go and see our parents.' He walked away, thinking Jess was following him.

But Jess was curious about Hector, so she stopped.

Perhaps he wasn't such a bad bird after all?

She thought about all the terrible things he'd done, but then, she couldn't recall there being anything *that* terrible.

After all, it's not like he'd killed anyone…

Jess couldn't remember seeing or hearing about any of the younglings being eaten.

*That's strange.* She thought, as she stared at the broken eagle.

Maybe he was just homesick too.

She remembered the story about Hector being taken from his home and his family.

As she waddled around the chicken wire, the faint rustling and snapping of twigs on the ground woke Hector and he opened an eye. He saw a ball of brown and yellow feathers. His eye widened, then narrowed.

'You,' Hector said, glumly, as he tried to sit up. 'Come to gloat, Little Wing,' he said, as he slumped back down in his misery.

Jess puffed out her chest.

'No, I've come to save you,' she said firmly, and she started to pull the chicken wire off Hector's body.

Hector winced in pain with every movement.

It took half an hour before he was completely free of the wire. He had deep cuts and tears all over his body, and there was damage to his left wing and leg. He knew he wouldn't be able to fly for a few days, but he could still walk, so he shuffled towards the edge of the park with Jess trailing after him.

Hector turned to look at Jess.

'You can go now, Little Wing,' he said, quietly.

He stood there looking defeated, his wings drooped down.

Jess felt an overwhelming sense of sadness for him.

How would he survive on his own? Who would help him hide and get food?

He was such a big bird that he'd stand out wherever he went.

He'd surely die on his own or be captured by humans.

Jess's mind was made up.

'I'm not leaving you alone,' she said firmly.

Hector's eyes widened again, but he felt a tiny glimmer of hope deep in the pit of his stomach - just when he thought all the hope was gone.

'Suit yourself,' said Hector, but secretly he was happy to have Little Wing's company, it reminded him of past times, when he went hunting with his older daughters.

The entrance gates were just ahead of them. Hector made his way towards them, but Jess stopped and pulled him into some bushes.

'Quick, let's go this way,' she said.

Hector followed Jess into the bushes. When they were hidden by the leaves, they turned and watched as the human who'd been tracking Hector walked out of the gates with a tranquiliser gun in his hand.

Hector held his breath in terror. He watched as the man looked around, but he finally got into a truck and drove away.

Hector let out his breath in a sigh of relief.

'Was that the human that took you?' Jess asked, quietly. Hector nodded.

'Horrible man,' said Jess with a furrowed brow, 'at least you're free now.'

Hector was silent.

'Perhaps. But there are others who'll never be free of him,' he said, quietly.

As they walked away, Hector told Jess about the owl and the others. Jess's eyes widened when Hector told her that the owl had never been out of the castle since the day he was caught.

'What an awful life,' Jess said sadly.

Hector breathed a deep sigh, he felt guilty keeping Jess away from her home and family any longer.

'Turn around and go back home. Where I'm going is too dangerous for ducklings,' said Hector.

Jess opened her beak, but then thought the better of it. She nodded and disappeared behind the nearest tree.

Hector puffed his chest out and headed off on his own into the strange unknown.

But of course, he wasn't alone. Because Little Wing wouldn't be told what to do, ever. Jess secretly waddled after the injured eagle, her new friend, and onto their next adventure.

Back at the lake, the sky was pitch-black, and the remaining younglings were being reunited with their parents one by one.

Prince George appeared and waddled over to the palace guards who were waiting for him. They stepped back to make way for his parents.

The King and Queen rushed over to Prince George and embraced him.

'My son!' cried the King.

He pulled back and looked at Prince George to check if he was hurt. When he could find no signs of injury, he hugged Prince George once again.

'I'm sorry for putting you down all the time,' said the King with a flurry of words. 'And for not believing in you. The Chief of Police told me how brave you were today. We're so very proud of you!' he finished as his emotions got the better of him.

Tears of joy slid down the Queen's cheeks. 'Yes. We're so happy to have you home!' she cried as she kissed her son's cheek.

'Jess! Jess!' came frantic voices.

Prince George turned to see Patrick and Anne frantically calling out Jess's name. He frowned.

'Would you wait here a second, please' he said to his parents.

The King and Queen watched with curiosity as their son walked over to the Mandarin Ducks.

'Excuse me, are you Jess Green's parents?' he asked. 'Yes! Have you seen her?' Patrick asked urgently.

'She was right behind me. I thought she came back here,' said the prince in a concerned tone.

'No, no! We haven't seen her!' Anne cried out.

'We went to the trap to see what happened to the eagle. I assumed she'd gone home,' Prince George said with alarm.

'Don't worry Mr and Mrs Green, we'll find your daughter.' Prince George reassured them, and then he hurried over to Quackovitz.

The King turned to the Queen.

'He's becoming a leader,' he said proudly.

When Prince George returned, they started to walk back

to the palace but a flash of white caught the Queen's eye. She looked down and touched one of Prince George's tail feathers.

It was turning white.

The Queen looked at the King and they smiled together.

When news of Jess being missing reached Goldie, Manny and the M.I.DIVE, they shot over to the trap with Anne and Patrick. But they soon found out that the trap was empty, there was only chicken wire and some of Hector's feathers on the ground.

Goldie and Manny searched the area until they found one of Jess's feathers in the mud. Goldie held it up.

Anne and Patrick cried and clung to one another when they saw it.

'That's our Jess's!' said Patrick.

'Oh! What's happened to her?' cried Anne.

Goldie looked down at the feather, then at Manny and the M.I.DIVE with a sinking heart.

He uttered some quacks of reassurance to the couple.

‘We’re going to find out what happened to Jess and we’re going to bring that eagle to justice,’ Goldie said firmly.

He and the others watched as Patrick and Anne clung to one another in sorrow.

Goldie turned the feather over, then stared up at the black sky, ready to complete his mission.

‘It shouldn’t be hard to find him, now that the storm’s stopped,’ said Manny. ‘He won’t get far if he’s injured.’

Goldie looked at Manny and the others. ‘That’s what I’m counting on. The storm may be over, but another’s just beginning,’ he said with grim determination.

**TO BE CONTINUED…**

# ABOUT THE AUTHORS

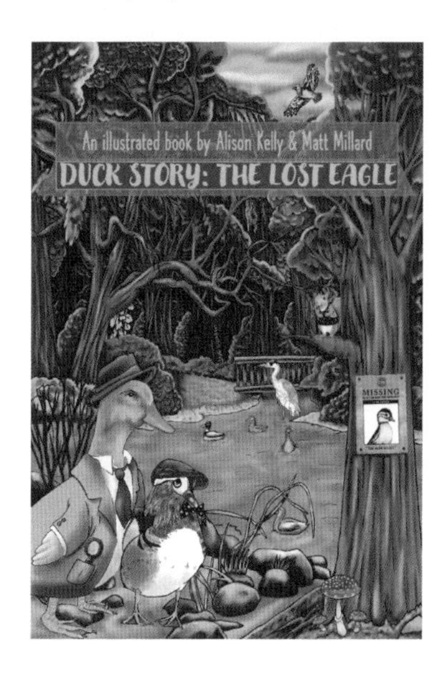


**Alison Kelly** and **Matt Millard** from Beckenham, Kent have recently finished writing *Duck Story: The Lost Eagle*, the first in a series of animal detective books set in parks across the UK. The book features two duck detectives, a Harpy eagle and elite birds of prey team the M.I.DIVE. Many of the characters are based on real-life animals from a park in Beckenham, Kent – Kelsey Park.

Alison studied directing at UCLA and has worked on several award-winning short films. She is currently working on *Bad Magic*, the first in a series of young adult books set in a world where magic has been banned and a boy, who isn't a wizard, finds the last wand in existence.

Matt is a budding actor who has had extra roles in *Alice in Wonderland: Through the Looking Glass, Criminal, Games of Thrones Prequel* and *Assassin's Creed.*

https://www.instagram.com/duckstorybooks/

# ABOUT THE ILLUSTRATOR

We'd like to give a big Thank You to our wonderful illustrator, Sabina, for the incredible, colourful illustrations she created to bring the animals and the story to life!!

**Sabina Anjum**
Illustrations and Cartoon Design artist

Contact details:
artisticqueen786@gmail.com
https://www.freelancer.com/u/ArtisticQueens
Whatsapp: +923244206942

## Kelsey Park

Matt and Alison were born in Beckenham, Kent. The book is set in their local park, Kelsey Park which is full of wonderful plants, trees and wildlife. Their ideas came from the many walks they took there during the lockdowns in 2020.

***Where the idea for Goldie came from***:

One of our favourite ducks in the park was a male, golden duck we saw between April 2018 and December 2019. We always looked out for him and gave him food each time we visited the park. He had this presence about him, and he always came over to us, but he seemed like a lonely duck. All the other ducks were in couples, but he was always alone, which is why we made sure to always give him attention. At the end of 2019, he suddenly disappeared, and we wondered what had happened to him.

Stumpy the squirrel is a fruit and nut trader, who lives in a high-rise tree.

Although he only has half a tail, he uses it to his advantage and has worked his way up to being a valued informant for Detective Goldie and the Pond Police.

Stumpy's tail was injured in an impossible mission that only he could complete.

In early 2020, another duck caught our eye, a very rare, gold female Mandarin duck. A few weeks later, we were delighted when we visited the park one morning and saw that she and her mate, a male Mandarin, had a little brown and yellow speckled duckling. It was so adorable, it followed them everywhere, zipping through the water.

A few weeks later, we went back to find the little duck family. They'd made a nest by the bridge on top of a sunken wooden log. We spotted the female and her mate straight away but alas there was no baby duckling :(

We have seen herons stalking the area, but will never know, what happened to it.

Although the ducks and other animals in the park come and go, every now and then we're lucky enough to catch a glimpse of one that takes a special place in our hearts. By making this book, we feel we're immortalising the golden duck and the little duckling.

# ACKNOWLEDGEMENTS

With grateful thanks for the support from the following:

Our Family & Friends

Bromley Council

Wendy Hardy & the Friends of Kelsey Park

Jackie Andrews & the Beckenham Appreciation Group

Waitrose & Partners

The Giggling Squid

Fiona Combe

Daniel Steward

Enrique & Cori Diaz

Tony Kamenick

Andrew Morris

## In loving memory of

# Marcus Emilio Diaz

Who soared high and is much loved and missed by his parents, Enrique and Cori Diaz, sister Jasmine, and family and friends.

# Donald "Donny" Fostner

Wise beyond his years, Donny will be greatly missed by his family and friends.

**Duck Story: The Lost Eagle**

In an inner-city park, Goldie, a duck detective who works for the **Pond Police**, is on the hunt for a thief who's been stealing ducklings, and the Swan King and Queen's eldest cygnet, Prince George.

After a mysterious eagle is spotted in the park, Goldie and his new partner, Manny the Mandarin duck, must work together to unravel the mystery with the help of the elite birds of prey team; the **M.I.DIVE**.

**Alison Kelly** and **Matt Millard** are authors from Kent who have recently finished writing *Duck Story: The Lost Eagle*, the first in a series of children's illustrated books featuring a duck detective and other animals, and the many adventures they have. The book series is set in different parks and nature spots across the UK.

Printed in Great Britain
by Amazon

21525601R00078